Seven
Little Rabbits

by John Becker

Illustrated by
Barbara Cooney

Scholastic Inc.
New York Toronto London Auckland Sydney Tokyo

ISBN 0-590-33447-6

12 11 10 9 8 7 6 5 4 3 2 1   10   4 5 6 7 8 9/8

Printed in the U.S.A.   09

Seven little rabbits
Walkin' down the road
Walkin' down the road

       Seven little rabbits
       Walkin' down the road
       To call on old friend toad.

One little rabbit
Said he was tired
Walkin' down the road
Walkin' down the road
One little rabbit
Said he was tired
Walkin' down the road
To call on old friend toad.

So
Seven little rabbits
Turned around
Until they found
Down in the ground
A hole
Built by a mole.

Here's somebody's house!

Let's investigate.

Seven little rabbits
Went down the hole
Built by the mole
Down in the ground
Until they found
A den.

Then
The seventh little rabbit
Went to sleep—
Shh, don't say "Peep"—
He's tucked in bed
And now, instead,
    There are . . .

Six little rabbits
Walkin' down the road
Walkin' down the road
Six little rabbits
Walkin' down the road
To call on old friend toad.

One little rabbit
Said he was tired
Walkin' down the road
Walkin' down the road
One little rabbit
Said he was tired
Walkin' down the road
To call on old friend toad.

Ho-hum. Let's go back to Mole's.

Let's take Toad some flowers.

So,
Six little rabbits
Turned around
Until they found
Down in the ground
A hole
Built by a mole.

Six little rabbits
Went down the hole
Built by the mole
Down in the ground
Until they found
A den.

Then
The sixth little rabbit
Went to sleep—
Shh, don't say "Peep"—
He's tucked in bed
And now, instead,
There are . . .

Five little rabbits
Walkin' down the road
Walkin' down the road
Five little rabbits
Walkin' down the road
To call on old friend toad.

One little rabbit
Said she was tired
Walkin' down the road
Walkin' down the road
One little rabbit
Said she was tired
Walkin' down the road
To call on old friend toad.

So
Five little rabbits
Turned around
Until they found
Down in the ground
A hole
Built by a mole.

Five little rabbits
Went down the hole
Built by the mole
Down in the ground
Until they found
A den.

Then
The fifth little rabbit
Went to sleep—
Shh, don't say "Peep"—
She's tucked in bed
And now, instead,
There are . . .

Four little rabbits
Walkin' down the road
Walkin' down the road
Four little rabbits
Walkin' down the road
To call on old friend toad.

One little rabbit
Said she was tired
Walkin' down the road
Walkin' down the road
One little rabbit
Said she was tired
Walkin' down the road
To call on old friend toad.

No wonder!
A blister. I'll get
you a band-aid.

So
Four little rabbits
Turned around
Until they found
Down in the ground
A hole
Built by a mole.

Four little rabbits
Went down the hole
Built by the mole
Down in the ground
Until they found
A den.

Then
The fourth little rabbit
Went to sleep—
Shh, don't say "Peep"—
She's tucked in bed
And now, instead,
There are . . .

Three little rabbits
Walkin' down the road
Walkin' down the road
Three little rabbits
Walkin' down the road
To call on old friend toad.

One little rabbit
Said she was tired
Walkin' down the road
Walkin' down the road
One little rabbit
Said she was tired
Walkin' down the road
To call on old friend toad.

Would you like
a chocolate-chip cookie
before going to bed?

So
Three little rabbits
Turned around
Until they found
Down in the ground
A hole
Built by a mole.

Three little rabbits
Went down the hole
Built by the mole
Down in the ground
Until they found
A den.

Then
The third little rabbit
Went to sleep—
Shh, don't say "Peep"—
She's tucked in bed
And now, instead,
There are . . .

Two little rabbits
Walkin' down the road
Walkin' down the road
Two little rabbits
Walkin' down the road
To call on old friend toad.

One little rabbit
Said he was tired
Walkin' down the road
Walkin' down the road
One little rabbit
Said he was tired
Walkin' down the road
To call on old friend toad.

Have you put on weight lately?

So
Two little rabbits
Turned around
Until they found
Down in the ground
A hole
Built by a mole.

Two little rabbits
Went down the hole
Built by the mole
Down in the ground
Until they found
A den.

Then
The second little rabbit
Went to sleep—
Shh, don't say "Peep"—
He's tucked in bed
And now, instead,
There is . . .

One little rabbit
Walkin' down the road
Walkin' down the road
One little rabbit
Walkin' down the road
To call on old friend toad.

One little rabbit
Said he was tired
Walkin' down the road
Walkin' down the road
One little rabbit
Said he was tired
Walkin' down the road
To call on old friend toad.

So
One little rabbit
Turned around
Until he found
Down in the ground
A hole
Built by a mole.

Then
The last little rabbit
Went to sleep—
Shh, don't say "Peep"—
He's tucked in bed
And now, instead,
Of walkin' down the road
Of walkin' down the road

The last little rabbit
Dreamed a dream
And in that dream
All in a blur
There were . . .

Seven little rabbits
Walkin' down the road
Walkin' down the road

Seven little rabbits
Walkin' down the road
To call on old friend toad.